williambee

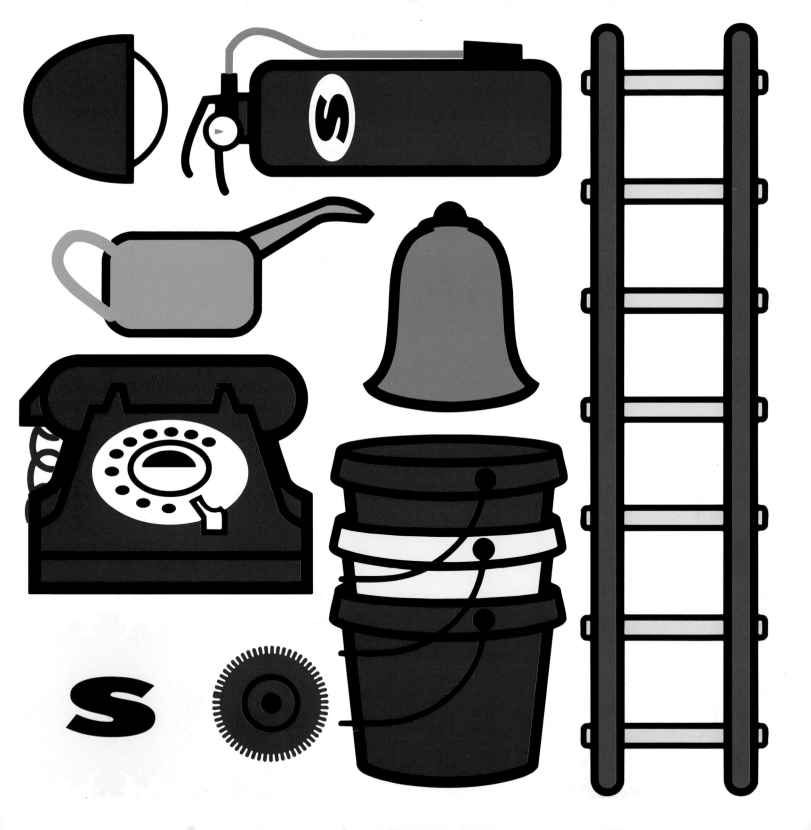

Ω

Published by
PEACHTREE PUBLISHING COMPANY INC.
1700 Chattahoochee Avenue
Atlanta, Georgia 30318-2112
www.peachtree-online.com

First published in Great Britain in 2020 by Jonathan Cape, an imprint of Penguin Random House Children's
First United States version published in 2020 by Peachtree Publishing Company Inc.

The illustrations were rendered digitally.

Printed in February 2020 by Tien Wah Press in Malaysia
10 9 8 7 6 5 4 3 2 1
First Edition

ISBN: 978-1-68263-214-7

Cataloging-in-Publication Data is available from the Library of Congress.

williambee
Stanley's
Fire Engine

PEACHTREE
ATLANTA

It's going to be another busy day
at Stanley's Fire Station.

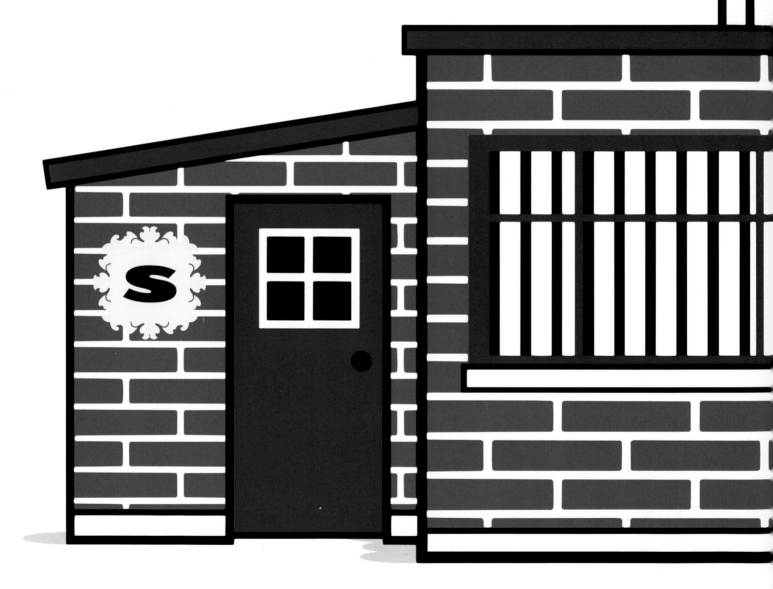

Stanley and Peggy keep
Stanley's fire engine in
tip-top condition.

It needs to be ready for anything!

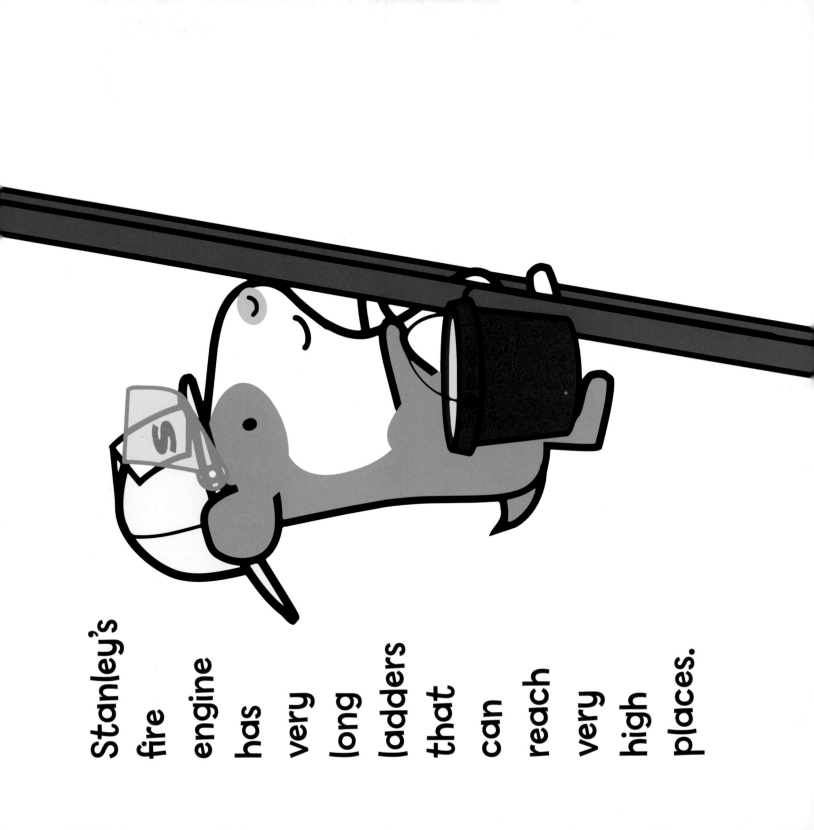

Stanley's fire engine has very long ladders that can reach very high places.

Like the tops of trees for whenever
kites and teddies and Little Woos
get stuck up them.

Stanley's fire engine also has
VERY long hoses.

They're perfect for extinguishing
Charlie's annual barbecue . . .

or cooling down anyone on
the sunniest of days.

CLANG! CLANG! CLANG! goes the bell.

Which means "GET OUT OF THE WAY!"
We're going to the . . .

FIREWORKS!
Stanley and Peggy stand by
in case of accidents.

But Shamus and Hattie know what they are doing, so everything goes off with—

a bang, a whizz, a swoosh, and a
KABOOM!

Well! What a busy day!

Stanley's
House

Time for supper!
Time for a bath!

And time for bed!
Goodnight, Stanley.

Stanley

If you liked **Stanley's Fire Engine** then you'll love these other books about Stanley:

Stanley the Builder
HC: $14.95 / 978-1-56145-801-1

Stanley the Farmer
HC: $14.95 / 978-1-56145-803-5

Stanley the Mailman
HC: $14.95 / 978-1-56145-867-7

Stanley's Diner
HC: $14.95 / 978-1-56145-802-8

Stanley's Garage
HC: $14.95 / 978-1-56145-804-2

Stanley's School
HC: $14.95 / 978-1-68263-070-9

Stanley's Store
HC: $14.95 / 978-1-56145-868-4

Stanley's Train
HC: $14.95 / 978-1-68263-108-9

williambee